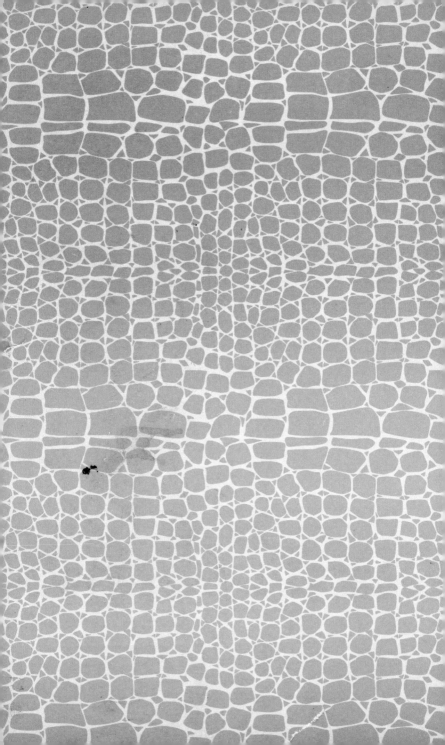

First published in Great Britain 2019 by Red Shed,
an imprint of Egmont UK Ltd
The Yellow Building, 1 Nicholas Road, London W11 4AN

www.egmont.co.uk
Copyright © Egmont UK 2019

Written by Rachel Moss
Illustrations by iStock.com /alashi; ambassador806; Ani_Ka; bubaone; Bullet_Chained; CSA-Archive;
Daria Voskoboeva; eduardrobert; ekmelica; IvanNikulin; jemastock; /lightkitegirl; MchlSkhrv; n_chetkova;
olando_o; sabelskaya; tanika84; Tribalium; vabadov; Vectorios2016; Victor_85

ISBN 978 1 4052 9604 5

A CIP catalogue record for this title is available from the British Library.

Egmont takes its responsibility to the planet and its inhabitants very seriously.
We aim to use papers from well-managed forests run by responsible suppliers.

The Ultimate
DRAGON
JOKE BOOK

ROAARRRR!

Welcome to my magical cave. I'm the scaliest, scariest, most hilarious dragon in the whole kingdom. My jokes are off the scales! Can you tell a funnier joke than me? Fire into these clawsome jokes and see if you can make your family and friends roar with laughter!

(Any jokes that don't make you laugh were probably written by knights!)

How do you know if there is a dragon in your refrigerator?

The door won't shut.

How do you raise a
baby dragon?

With a forklift truck.

What game do dragons
like to play with humans?

Squash.

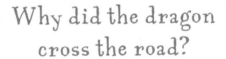

Why did the dragon
cross the road?

*To eat the princess
on the other side.*

How do you keep
dragons out of a castle
made of cheese?

Moatzarella.

Why did the dragon
cross the road again?

*It was the chicken's
day off.*

How long
does it take a
dragon to blow out
the candles on their
birthday cake?

FOREVER.

Why do dragons
snooze during
the day?

So they can fight knights.

How do you train
a dragon?

Buy it a ticket from the station.

What do you do when a
dragon blows its nose?

Use a shield!

What's scarier than a dragon?

TWO dragons.

How do you greet a dragon as tall as a house, with long, pointy teeth and claws?

Politely. And call him Sir, so he doesn't eat you!

What do you call a dragon
wearing headphones?

Anything you like, he won't hear you.

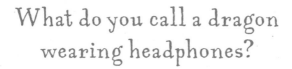

What's as big
as a dragon but
weighs nothing?

Its shadow.

What does a dragon
call a porcupine?

A toothbrush!

Why aren't dragons
allowed on the ice
hockey team?

They keep melting the ice.

What do
dragons eat for
breakfast?

Toast.

What do you call two
dragons on a bicycle?

Optimistic.

How many
dragons does it
take to change a
light bulb?

*Don't be silly, dragons
can't change light bulbs.*

How would you know
if there was a dragon
under your bed?

*Your nose would be
touching the ceiling.*

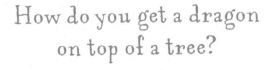

How do you get a dragon
on top of a tree?

*Stand her on an acorn and wait
fifty years!*

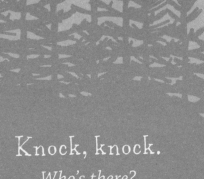

Knock, knock.
Who's there?
Interrupting
dragon.
Interrupting dra–
ROAR!

Why did the dragon
get sent to its room?

Bad altitude.

What sound do you hear when dragons eat chillies?

A fire alarm!

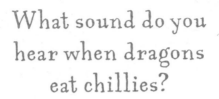

Knock, knock.
Who's there?
Fire.
Fire who?
Fire were you,
I'd keep away from
dragons.

Why should you take a dragon camping?

They always light the campfire.

What's a dragon's favourite day of the week?

Chewsday.

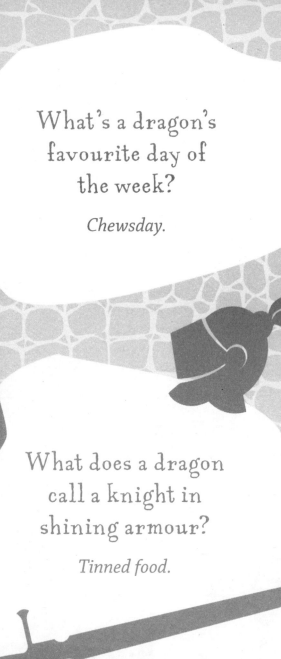

What does a dragon call a knight in shining armour?

Tinned food.

Why are dragons
easy to weigh?

Because they have their own scales.

What do you call
a dragon that can
juggle?

Talon-ted.

What do dragons have nightmares about?

Children under the bed!

What do you call a man who
upsets a dragon?

Ash.

What did the dragon say
when he got excited?

I'm all fired up!

What does a dragon say
at Halloween?

*Treat! Or I'll burn your
house down.*

What's the difference between an ice cream and a dragon?

If you don't know, then I'm never asking you to get me an ice cream.

What time did the
dragon go to the
dentist?

Tooth-hurty o'clock.

Why did the dragon
run out of the cave?

*He was
claws-trophobic.*

What's the difference between an English dragon and an Australian dragon?

About 9,000km.

What happened to the dragon's assistant?

He got fired.

Why didn't the dragon
eat the pirate ship?

Its cannons had gone off.

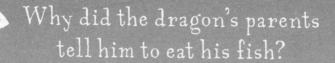 Why did the dragon's parents
tell him to eat his fish?

They said it was good for his scales.

What do sea dragons eat?

Fish and ships.

What is a sea dragon's favourite food?

Smoked salmon.

What do you call a dragon who can't fly?

Late.

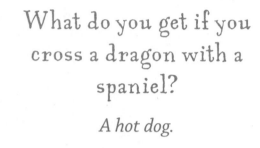

What do you get if you
cross a dragon with a
spaniel?

A hot dog.

What's green and
scaly with four
wheels?

*A dragon riding
a tractor.*

What do you call a dragon in a phone box?

Stuck.

Why are dragons
so grumpy?

They have very hot tempers.

What did the dragon say
about his birthday party?

'That was a knight to remember.'

What's green and scaly
and has two wheels?

A dragon riding a scooter.

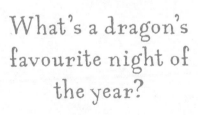

What's a dragon's
favourite night of
the year?

Bonfire night.

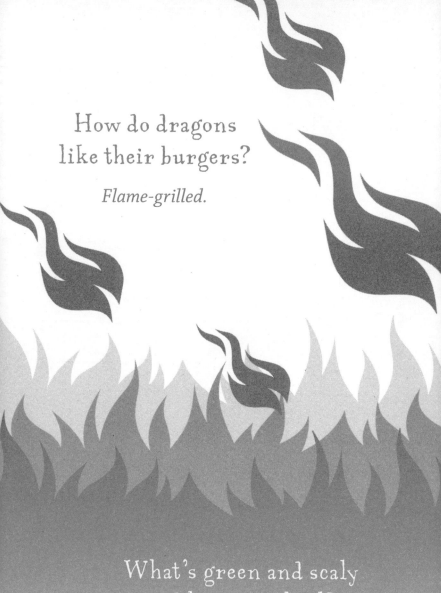

How do dragons
like their burgers?

Flame-grilled.

What's green and scaly
and has one wheel?

A dragon riding a unicycle.

What did the dragon like
best about school?

Fire drills.

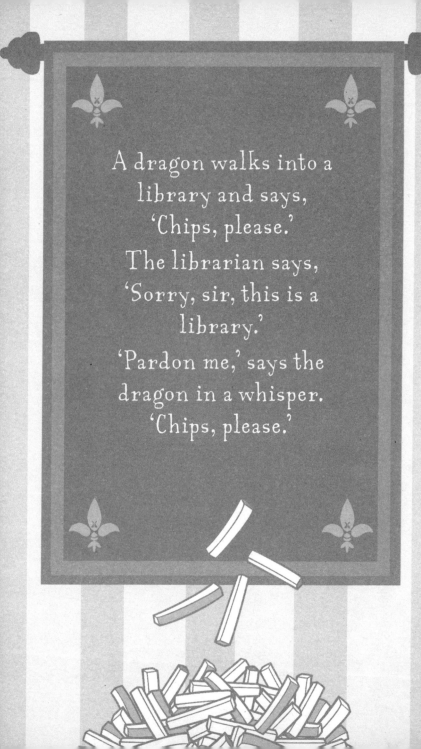

What does a baby
dragon cover herself
with at night?

A fire blanket.

Knock knock!

Who's there?
Fangs.

Fangs who?
Fangs for
inviting me.

Why did the dragon
say 'neigh'?

*She was learning
a new language.*

What did the baby
dragon say at bedtime?

Knight knight.

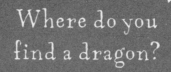

Where do you
find a dragon?

It depends where you left it!

What do dragons do
when they don't want to
go for a walk?

DRAG their heels.

What do you call a dragon that's not where you left it?

Dra-gone!

Why did the dragon
carry the prince in
her mouth?

*Because she didn't
have any pockets.*

What do you call a
dragon with a spade
on his head?

Doug.

What do you call a dragon
without a spade on his head?

Douglas.
(Geddit? Doug-less!)

What goes up very slowly and comes down very fast?

A dragon in a lift.

How do dragons measure things?

On a scale of one to ten.

What is a
dragon's
favourite job?

*Travelling
scalesman.*

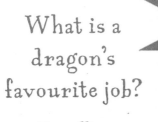

Why did the dragon
go for a swim?

To let off steam.

What do you
give a dragon
that's upset?

Whatever it wants.

Why don't dragons
like penguins?

*Because they can't get the
wrappers off.*

What should you do
if you find a dragon
in your bed?

Sleep somewhere else.

Why wouldn't the
dragon put the kettle on?

Because it didn't fit.

Why did the dragon
wear a clock on his head?

He wanted to make time fly.

What turns from green to red?

An embarrassed dragon.

What do dragons do to relax?

They just blaze around.

Why did the dragon visit the village?

He wanted a bite to eat.

What came after the dragon lit her birthday candles?

Fire engines!

Why shouldn't
you tease
dragon eggs?

*They can't
take a yolk.*

Why did the
dragon sit on
her eggs?

*Because she didn't
have any chairs.*

Which day did the
dragon go hunting?

Fry-day.

Why did the dragon
spit out the clown?

Because he tasted funny.

Can a dragon jump
higher than a
mountain?

*Of course! Mountains
can't jump.*

What do
dragons use to
see in the dark?

Knight lights.

If storks deliver baby
boys and girls, which
birds deliver baby
dragons?

Cranes.

What did the little dragon say after the sleepover?

'Fang you for having me.'

Where did knights learn how to fight dragons?

Night school.

What always
follows a dragon?

Its tail.

What's bright red, weighs
five tons and has smoke
coming out of its ears?

A dragon holding its breath.

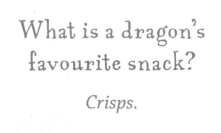

What is a dragon's favourite snack?

Crisps.

Why do dragons hoard their treasure?

The shopkeepers won't let them in to spend it.

How does a
dragon like his
vegetables?

RAW!

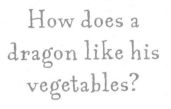

How did the octopus win
the battle against the dragon?

He was well-armed.

Knock Knock!

Who's there?

Dragon.

Dragon who?

Knock Knock!

Who's there?

Dragon.

Dragon who?

Knock Knock!

Who's there?

Dragon.

Dragon who?

Knock Knock!

Who's there?

Aunt.

Aunt who?

Aunt you glad the
dragon's gone?

Why did the dragon
sleep in the day?

She was working a night shift.

What do dragons
say when they see
the ice rink?

'Fancy a swim?'

What did the little
dragon want to be
when he grew up?

Flamous.

Why didn't anyone take
the dragon seriously?

He was full of hot air.

What do you call a
bad-tempered dragon?

Roary.

Which part of a
dragon weighs
the most?

The scales.

Why didn't the dragons eat
the cows on the hilltop?

*The steaks were
too high.*

Why was the little dragon
rude to her friend?

She spoke in the heat of the moment.

What do
you get if you put
a dragon in the
fireplace?

Fireworks.

Did you hear about the dragon actor who forgot his lines?

He had to wing it.

What did the tree say to the dragon?

Nothing – trees can't talk.

How did the
dragon get into
university?

She was a bright spark.

Why are dragons
such bad dancers?

Because they have two left feet.

Did you hear about the
dragon party?

It was a roaring success.

Why did the cowardly
dragon go to bed early?

*Because he didn't want
to see the knight.*

Why don't parents like this book?

The jokes drag-on too long.

What do dragons compete in?

Talon shows.

Why was the dragon
bored at school?

*The teacher kept dragging
on and on and on!*

Why are dragons
great pianists?

*They really know
their scales.*

Did you hear about the guy who did amazing dance moves with his dragon?

He was on fire!

What is a dragon's favourite toy?

Scalectrics.

What did the dragon
say to the witch when
she tried to pinch
his cheese?

That's nacho cheese!

Why did the
dragon not need to
go to the dentist?

He was toothless.

Why did the wizard
get better school grades
than the dragon?

He was better at spelling!

Why did the dragon
visit the queen?

To be knighted.

What did the dragon
wear to the disco?

Hot pants.

What do hungry
dragons call a knight?

Dinner!

What do you
get if you take a
dragon into the city?

Free parking.

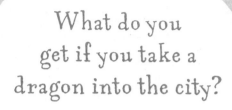

What's the
difference between a
car and a dragon?

A car only has one horn.

When do dragons
do their shopping?

In the January scales.

Why did the
dragon do so well
in school?

*Because he was the
teacher's pet.*

What time is it when a
dragon sits on your car?

Time to get a new car.

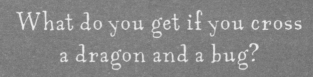

What do you get if you cross a dragon and a bug?

A dragonfly!

What happened when
the dragon met his
long-lost sister?

They got on like a house on fire.

What is a dragon's
favourite instrument?

A tromBONE.

Why is the sky so high?

So dragons don't bang their heads.

Where do dragons keep their clothes?

In the clawset.

Knock, knock.

Who's there?

Dragon.

Dragon who?

Dragon your feet again?